My Best Friend Is Cinderella

By Lisa Ann Marsoli

Illustrated by the Disney Storybook Artists

Random House 🏠 New York

Copyright © 2006 Disney Enterprises, Inc. All rights reserved. Published in the United States by Random House Children's Books, a division of Random House, Inc., New York, in conjunction with Disney Enterprises, Inc.

RANDOM HOUSE and the Random House colophon are registered trademarks of Random House, Inc.

Library of Congress Control Number: 2005928296

ISBN: 0-7364-2389-3

www.randomhouse.com/kids/disney

MANUFACTURED IN CHINA   10 9 8 7 6 5 4 3 2 1

"The princess is coming!" the girls exclaimed as they watched Cinderella's carriage come down the hill.

"Let me see! Let me see!" cried little Emma, who had arrived at the girls' school only a few days before.

As Emma peered out the window, she saw the fancy coach come to a stop right outside the school. It was so close that Emma could see the jewels on the horses' bridles sparkling in the sun!

"Quickly, girls, gather around," said the headmistress. She scurried to the door and opened it wide.

"Welcome, Your Highness!" the headmistress exclaimed. All the little girls curtsied.

"Thank you!" said Cinderella. "It's so nice to see you all again."

Cinderella often visited the school to help the girls with their reading and writing. She also brought books, clothes, and toys to the ones who had few things of their own.

All the girls were happy to see Cinderella. But no one was as thrilled as little Emma.

Cinderella and the girls spent a wonderful afternoon together. When it was time for her to go, she made an announcement:

"In one week, there will be a grand ball held in your honor at the castle. And I am having dresses, shoes, and gloves made for each of you!"

"Thank you, Princess Cinderella!" the girls shouted in excitement.

For the next few days, the girls talked about nothing but the party. The headmistress decided they needed a distraction.

"It's a lovely day," she announced. "Let's go have a picnic."

As the other children ran and played, Emma sat and gazed at the castle. "I can't wait to see what it looks like inside," she said to herself. "It must be the most wonderful place in the world."

Soon Emma noticed a group of seamstresses approaching the castle. *Hmm,* she thought, *maybe I can peek at the courtyard when they go inside.* She quickly ran to the gates and hid.

But when the gates opened, Emma was so excited that she followed the women straight through the courtyard—and into the castle!

Emma couldn't believe she was inside Cinderella's castle! It was even more beautiful than she had imagined.

She hid behind a velvet curtain as she watched the princess lead the seamstresses up a sweeping staircase. Just when Emma thought the coast was clear, she noticed two little mice looking at her. Uh-oh!

Luckily, the nice mice didn't tell on her. Jaq and Gus introduced themselves and then led Emma upstairs to explore more of the castle.

Another mouse, Mary, joined them as Emma admired a lovely bedroom with a pink ruffled canopy bed. "I'd surely have sweet dreams if I slept here," Emma whispered to her new friends.

Suddenly, they heard a voice from down the hall: "This fabric is exquisite!"

Emma and the mice tiptoed over and peeked through a doorway. The room was filled with bolts of satin, silk, and velvet. In the center of it all, the seamstresses were hard at work.

Emma couldn't stay quiet any longer. "It's all so pretty!" she blurted out.

"Come in! Come in!" the seamstresses called to her. They thought Cinderella had sent Emma to model the dresses!

Emma smiled as they draped her in soft fabrics.

When Cinderella looked in awhile later, Emma was barely visible beneath all the satin, ruffles, and lace. "More bows, please," Emma requested.

"Oh, my!" exclaimed Cinderella. "That certainly is a fancy dress!"

Cinderella thought Emma had come with the seamstresses! So as the dressmakers continued their work, the princess invited Emma to have a snack with her.

"I've never met anyone as pretty as you before," Emma told Cinderella.

Cinderella laughed. "That's very kind of you to say," she replied.

"It must be wonderful to be a princess," Emma said. "You get to wear fancy clothes and live in a big castle."

Cinderella smiled. "There's much more to being a princess than castles and nice clothes. Why don't you help me this afternoon and see what a princess *really* does?"

For the next few hours, Emma and Cinderella put together baskets of clothing, books, and toys for schools and orphanages around the kingdom. Emma's favorite part was going through Cinderella's wardrobe to look for old clothes that could be donated.

She tried on a velvet cape and hat and twirled around.

"You look positively stunning!" said Cinderella, laughing.

Soon it was time to deliver the baskets. Emma climbed into the royal carriage beside Cinderella. As they rode through the village, the little girl leaned out the window and waved at the passersby.

Princess Emma, she thought. *I like the sound of that!*

When they arrived at the girls' school, the headmistress gave Emma a big hug.

"Where have you been?" she cried. "We've been so worried."

"But I thought she arrived with the seamstresses," Cinderella said, puzzled.

"I'm sorry," Emma said, and she explained everything. "I didn't mean to make anyone worry. I just wanted to see what it was like to be a princess."

"Why don't you help me each day when you've finished your studies?" Cinderella suggested. "Then you can learn more about what a princess really does."

"I'd love to," Emma said.

After that, Emma spent her afternoons watching Cinderella run the castle and work with charities. She saw that being a princess wasn't easy, and she admired Cinderella even more.

Emma's favorite princess task was helping to plan the girls' party. "May we serve little cakes with pink icing?" Emma asked. "The girls love pink icing!"

"Of course," answered Cinderella. "You're a very thoughtful friend."

Finally, the night of the ball arrived. The girls twirled across the dance floor in their magnificent new dresses.

"I still wish I could be a real princess," said Emma.

"You're a real *friend,*" replied Cinderella, "and that's what matters most of all."